HOWARD THE AVERAGE GECKO

Published by
PEACHTREE PUBLISHING COMPANY INC.
1700 Chattahoochee Avenue
Atlanta, Georgia 30318-2112
PeachtreeBooks.com

Text © 2021 by Wendy Meddour
Illustrations © 2021 by Carmen Saldaña

First published in the United Kingdom in 2021 by Oxford University Press.
First United States version published in 2022 by Peachtree Publishing Company Inc.

The illustrations were rendered in watercolor, pencil, and digital.

Printed in March 2022 in China
10 9 8 7 6 5 4 3 2 1
First Edition
ISBN 978-1-68263-434-9

Cataloging-in-Publication Data is available from the Library of Congress.

ldour   Carmen Saldaña

HOWARD THE
AVERAGE
GECKO

Ω

PEACHTREE

ATLANTA

Howard was very
proud of himself.

"I'm Howard
the Exceptional Gecko,"
he announced. "I'm the only
camouflaged creature
in the rain forest!"

"Ouch!"
said something
on the branch.

But Howard didn't notice.

"It's not easy being this special," sighed Howard.

"But what can I do?"

"Ribbit,"
croaked something
sitting on a log.

But Howard didn't notice.

"Look at me now . . . ,"
Howard said.

"And now . . .

and now!"

"I'm so brilliantly camouflaged that I deserve a prize."

Something fluttered around Howard's head and flew away.

But Howard didn't notice.

"They should call me
Howard the Camouflaged King
of the Rain Forest. Or maybe . . .
Howard the Camouflaged
King of the World!"

Something shook its antenna,
but Howard didn't notice.

"Come to think about it,"
said Howard, "I'm probably . . ."

"Oh, for goodness' sake!"

something said.

"Will you please give it a rest?"

Howard spun around.
But he didn't see
anyone else.

"Where are you?"
Howard asked.

"Over here,
you nincompoop!"
something said.

"Whooaah!" cried Howard.
"You're camouflaged too!"

"Of course I am," the creature said.
"I'm a stick insect."

"The rain forest is full of camouflaged creatures," the stick insect told Howard. "Bees, beetles, birds, butterflies . . . We're all here. You just don't notice us. You're too busy paying attention to yourself."

Howard groaned. "If I'm not the Camouflaged King of the Rain Forest, then what am I?"

"You're average,"
said the stick insect.

"Average!" gasped Howard.
"Howard the . . . Average?

"I can't just be average!"

"Why not?"
the stick insect
asked.

"Who will love me
if I'm just an
average gecko?"

Howard licked his
eyeballs and started to cry.

"I will," said a voice.

Howard blinked
and looked up.
"Who is that?"

"It's another average gecko,"
said the stick insect.
"Can't you see her?"

From out of the leaves came
the most beautiful creature that
Howard had ever seen.

Her skin was
wrinkly.
Her fingertips
were gloopy.

And her eyes wobbled about
like spinning moons.

Howard gulped.
"You're not average.
You're . . .
magnificent!"

"She *is* average,"
said the stick insect.

"I'm Dolores, actually," said Dolores,
flicking out her tongue and catching a fly.

"Blimey!"
said Howard.

Dolores
blushed.

"Would you like to watch the sunset from the treetops?" said Howard. "We could even turn orange together, if you'd like."

"Oh, go on then," said Dolores.
"I'll give it a try."

So, two average geckos
climbed up a tree and sat
on a big, furry branch
to watch the sunset.

Wait! What's that?
A big, furry branch?

"Whoops. Sorry!" giggled
Dolores and Howard.

Snake

Monkey

Owl

A gecko is a kind of lizard that is found on every continent but Antarctica. Some geckos can change their appearance, a process called camouflage, to blend in with their surroundings and hide from predators. Most geckos do not have eyelids, so they lick their own eyeballs to clean them.

Geckos are not the only animals who use camouflage. So can stick insects, like the one in this book. In fact, there are lots of other camouflaged creatures hiding in this book. How many can you spot?

Stick insect

Beetle

Ladybug

Butterfly

Frog